HENRI MOUSE

By George Mendoza
Pictures by Joelle Boucher

VIKING KESTREL

For many years, in New York City, Henry Mouse had a cheese store. He grew fat nibbling on this and that delicious cheese. And then he grew bored.

He decided to open a bookstore for children, a store devoted to selling books filled with mouse adventures. Henry Mouse called his little bookstore "Mouse Books." A bold sign over his shop read: NO CATS ALLOWED!

Henry Mouse loved all the children who came to his bookstore, but after a while he grew tired of so many look-alike mouse books. He decided once again that he would do something completely different with his life.

Henry Mouse was going to be an artist!

Henry sold his bookstore, packed his bags, and boarded a jumbo jet for Paris, for where else would a mouse go who wanted to be a serious artist?

Once in Paris, Henry Mouse changed his name to Henri Mouse and bought himself an easel, brushes, and many canvases on which to paint his pictures.

Then, following an ancient formula he had discovered in a book called *The Art of Mouse Masters,* he set about mixing special magnetic paints in all shades and colors.

He looked very much the artist, with his artist's smock, his huge black artist's beret, and his striking artist's pose.

No doubt about it, Henri Mouse *was* an artist, through and through.

Henri went all over Paris, painting scenes that caught his imagination. He painted the colorful flower and bird markets, the lovely statues in the Tuileries Gardens, the moody quays of the Left Bank, the wonderful boats and barges that cruised the Seine. He sketched landmarks, such as the Eiffel Tower and the majestic cathedral of Nôtre-Dame.

He made illustrations of the beautiful Bluebell Girls as they danced at the Lido nightclub.

Wherever he went he created a sensation, since he was without question the only mouse painter in Paris! And even more unusual, Henri was a magical painter. Somehow, with his magnetic paints, he managed to remove from real life everything that he painted, capturing forever that person, place, or thing on his canvas.

   If Henri Mouse painted the moon, good-bye moon! Good-bye everything painted by Henri Mouse.

Here, a bridge that Henri just painted has suddenly disappeared.

What a terrific traffic jam!

A small boy is sailing his favorite boat on the pond.
Then, like magic, the boat vanishes.

There is Henri, carrying it off.

Now Henri quickly sketches the front of a lovely house
and carries it off on his canvas.

How interesting to see what's inside!

Look out, grandmother! Henri Mouse, the artist,
is painting your sundae.

Just look at the happiness on all those smiling faces as they swirl
around on the carousel.

But where have all the animals gone?

Do you see that thief running away from a policeman?

Hurrah! Henri Mouse captures him on his new painting.

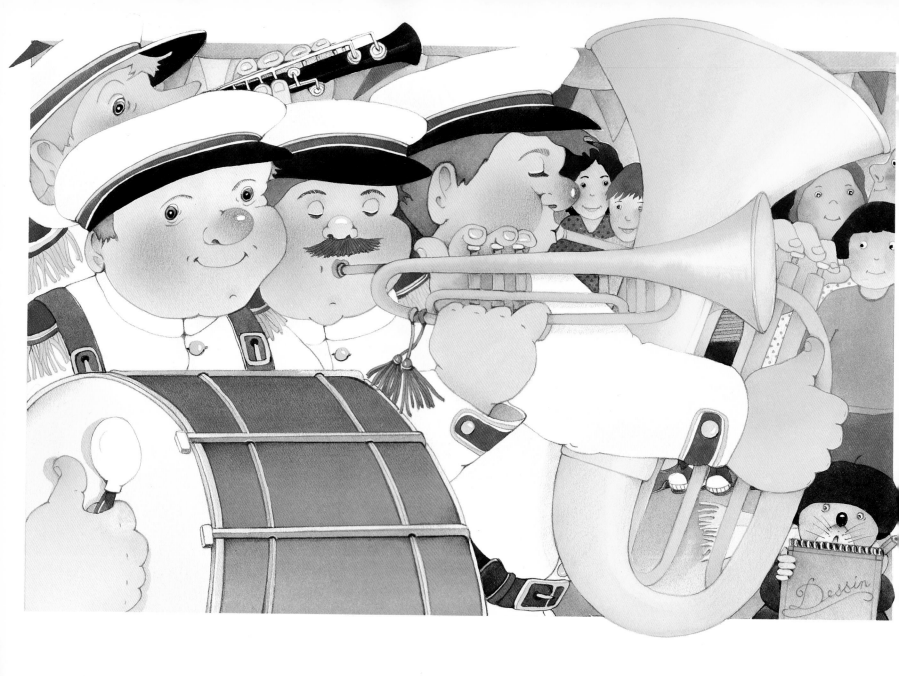

"What wonderful music!" exclaims Henri.

But what do musicians play when their instruments are painted away?

A very rich lady is about to enter her limousine as her chauffeur holds open the door.

Oops! Henri leaves her sitting on the ground.

"Ah," says Henri, "look at that pretty bird."
But you can see what he does now.

And here is Santa about to deliver toys to all the good children.
How can he do that without a chimney to climb down?

No, indeed, Henri Mouse was no ordinary artist. In fact, he was a menace.

But Henri didn't know what his magnetic paints were doing. He was too involved in his painting to notice.

Then one day Henri paid a visit to the Louvre. There he discovered that all the great masters had painted self-portraits. So of course Henri Mouse decided to paint himself.

It was a fine portrait, a perfect likeness of Henri Mouse.

But now, Henri Mouse had become his own painting!

Except for his tail, his arms, his legs, and his feet.

That might have been the end of Henri Mouse forever, had it not been for
a sudden rainstorm and the fact that his magnetic paints had not yet dried.

As you can see, Henri is back,
and who knows, he might be
thinking of painting you!

For Ashley and Ryan,
a little story from Paris
and from the heart…
G.M.

Pour mon petit Kenzo
J.B.

VIKING KESTREL
Viking Penguin Inc., 40 West 23rd Street, New York, New York 10010, U.S.A.
Penguin Books Ltd, Harmondsworth, Middlesex, England
Penguin Books Australia Ltd, Ringwood, Victoria, Australia
Penguin Books Canada Limited, 2801 John Street, Markham, Ontario, Canada L3R 1B4
Penguin Books (N.Z.) Ltd, 182–190 Wairau Road, Auckland 10, New Zealand

Text copyright © George Mendoza, 1985
Illustrations copyright © Joelle Boucher, 1985
All rights reserved

First published in 1985 by Viking Penguin Inc.
Published simultaneously in Canada

Library of Congress Cataloging in Publication Data
Mendoza, George.   Henri Mouse.
Summary: Henri Mouse goes to Paris to become an artist,
but causes much confusion when everything he paints disappears
and is magically transferred onto his canvas.
1. Children's stories, American.   [1. Mice—Fiction.
2. Artists—Fiction]   I. Boucher, Joelle, ill.   II. Title.
PZ7.M5255Hd 1985   [E]   84-19622   ISBN 0-670-36689-7

Printed in Japan by Dai Nippon
1   2   3   4   5   89   88   87   86   85
Set in Korinna.